D1443697

THE Mine-O-Saur

by **Sudipta Bardhan-Quallen** • illustrated by **David Clark**

G. P. Putnam's Sons

G. P. PUTNAM'S SONS
A division of Penguin Young Readers Group. Published by The Penguin Group.
Penguin Group (USA) Inc., 375 Hudson Street, New York, NY 10014, U.S.A.
Penguin Group (Canada), 90 Eglinton Avenue East, Suite 700, Toronto, Ontario, Canada M4P 2Y3
(a division of Pearson Penguin Canada Inc.).
Penguin Books Ltd, 80 Strand, London WC2R 0RL, England.
Penguin Ireland, 25 St. Stephen's Green, Dublin 2, Ireland (a division of Penguin Books Ltd.).
Penguin Group (Australia), 250 Camberwell Road, Camberwell, Victoria 3124, Australia
(a division of Pearson Australia Group Pty Ltd).
Penguin Books India Pvt Ltd, 11 Community Centre, Panchsheel Park, New Delhi - 110 017, India.
Penguin Group (NZ), 67 Apollo Drive, Mairangi Bay, Auckland 1311, New Zealand (a division of Pearson New Zealand Ltd).
Penguin Books (South Africa) (Pty) Ltd, 24 Sturdee Avenue, Rosebank, Johannesburg 2196, South Africa.
Penguin Books Ltd, Registered Offices: 80 Strand, London WC2R 0RL, England.

Library of Congress Cataloging-in-Publication Data

ISBN 978-0-399-24642-5

1 2 3 4 5 6 7 8 9 10
First Impression

To Mommy and Daddy,

who tried to teach me how to share.—S. B.-Q.

To Michael.—D.C.

One morning, before Mrs. Raptor rang the bell, the dinosaurs were playing in the school yard.

All of a sudden, they heard a roar: "MINE! MINE! MINE!"

"Oh, no," muttered Stegosaurus. "Here comes the Mine-o-saur."

He snatched the jump rope and the ball.
He threw the cars against the wall.
And then he roared to one and all,
"MINE! MINE! MINE!"

Iguanodon said, "That's not fair."
Triceratops said, "You should share."
But the Mine-o-saur yelled, "I don't care!
They're MINE! MINE! MINE!"

Right then, the bell rang. The Mine-o-saur hugged the toys and sighed, "All mine."

"You're late," Mrs. Raptor said when the Mine-o-saur finally came to class. "Now you'll have to paint your project during snack time."

By the time the Mine-o-saur finished,
snack time was in full swing.

The Mine-o-saur rushed on ahead.
He snatched the scones and strudel bread.
He bit the butter tarts and said,
"They're MINE! MINE! MINE!"

"That's our food!" yelled Apatosaur.
"No, it's not!" cried Mine-o-saur.

And soon there was a tug-of-war
As he wailed, "MINE!"

"The rest of the class can go out for recess," Mrs. Raptor said. "You will stay here until you clean up this mess."

The Mine-o-saur scowled and bit into a scone. "At least the food's all mine," he grumbled. But the feast wasn't as much fun when it was made for one.

At recess, the Mine-o-saur saw the other dinos having fun building a tower.

His arms were flailing all around.
The tower tumbled to the ground.
He grabbed a bunch of blocks and frowned.
"They're MINE! MINE! MINE!"

"How could you?" yelled Iguanodon.
"It's wrecked now!" said Pteranodon.
The Mine-o-saur said, "Oh, come on,
These blocks are MINE!"

The dinos rolled their eyes. Finally, Triceratops said, "Let's go, guys."

"I don't need them anyway," said the Mine-o-saur.
"I'll build a better tower by myself."

"Look at this!" he shouted. "The biggest tower ever!"
But there was no dino around to hear.

At the other end of the yard, the rest of the dinos were laughing and playing. They didn't seem to miss the Mine-o-saur at all.

The Mine-o-saur began to shake.
"There's nothing left for me to take!
No toys at all, for goodness' sake.
And they don't care!"

The Mine-o-saur wanted to laugh and play too. So he gathered up all the stuff that was his and headed toward the dinos.

The Mine-o-saur asked, "Want some snacks?"
The other dinos turned their backs.
"I've brought the blocks for us to stack.
Come on, let's share!"

The Mine-o-saur tried saying, "Please!
I've brought some toys—I'll give you these!"
The dinos stared down at their knees.
They just didn't care.

"Okay, then," said the Mine-o-saur. He put all the stuff down. "You guys should play."

The dinos looked at each other. "Isn't this YOUR stuff?" asked Stegosaurus.

The Mine-o-saur shook his head. "I shouldn't have taken it."

The Mine-o-saur was still walking when
he heard the dinos shout, "Wait!"

They said, "We want to play with you!"
Said Mine-o-saur, "You really do?"
The dinos nodded. "Yes, it's true.
If you'll share, it's fine."

The Mine-o-saur yelled, "It's a deal!
I have the thing I want," he squealed.
"You don't know how this makes me feel—
My friends! You're MINE!"